For the real K,
the real Mac,
and the real Woolyman,
who is still missing

Atheneum Books for Young Readers
An imprint of Simon & Schuster
Children's Publishing Division
1230 Avenue of the Americas
New York, New York 10020

Book design by Ann Bobco
The text for this book is handlettered
by Rainy Dohaney.
The illustrations for this book are
rendered in watercolor wash and
colored pencils.
Manufactured in China
First Edition
2 4 6 8 10 9 7 5 3 1
Library of Congress
Cataloging-in-Publication Data
Dohaney, Rainy.
My best sweet potato / Rainy Dohaney.— 1st ed.
p. cm.
Summary: A little girl cries and searches
frantically after a curious weaverbird carries away
Woolyman, her favorite toy friend.
ISBN-13: 978-0-689-86379-0 (ISBN-13)
ISBN-10: 0-689-86379-9 (ISBN-10)
[1. Stuffed animals (Toys)—Fiction.
2. Lost and found possessions—Fiction.]
I. Title.
PZ7.D69455Myab 2005
[E]—dc22 2005012614

Thanks to Karl Hauser, Jane Veeder, Rob Pike, Amanda, and to Anne, Ann, and Annie.

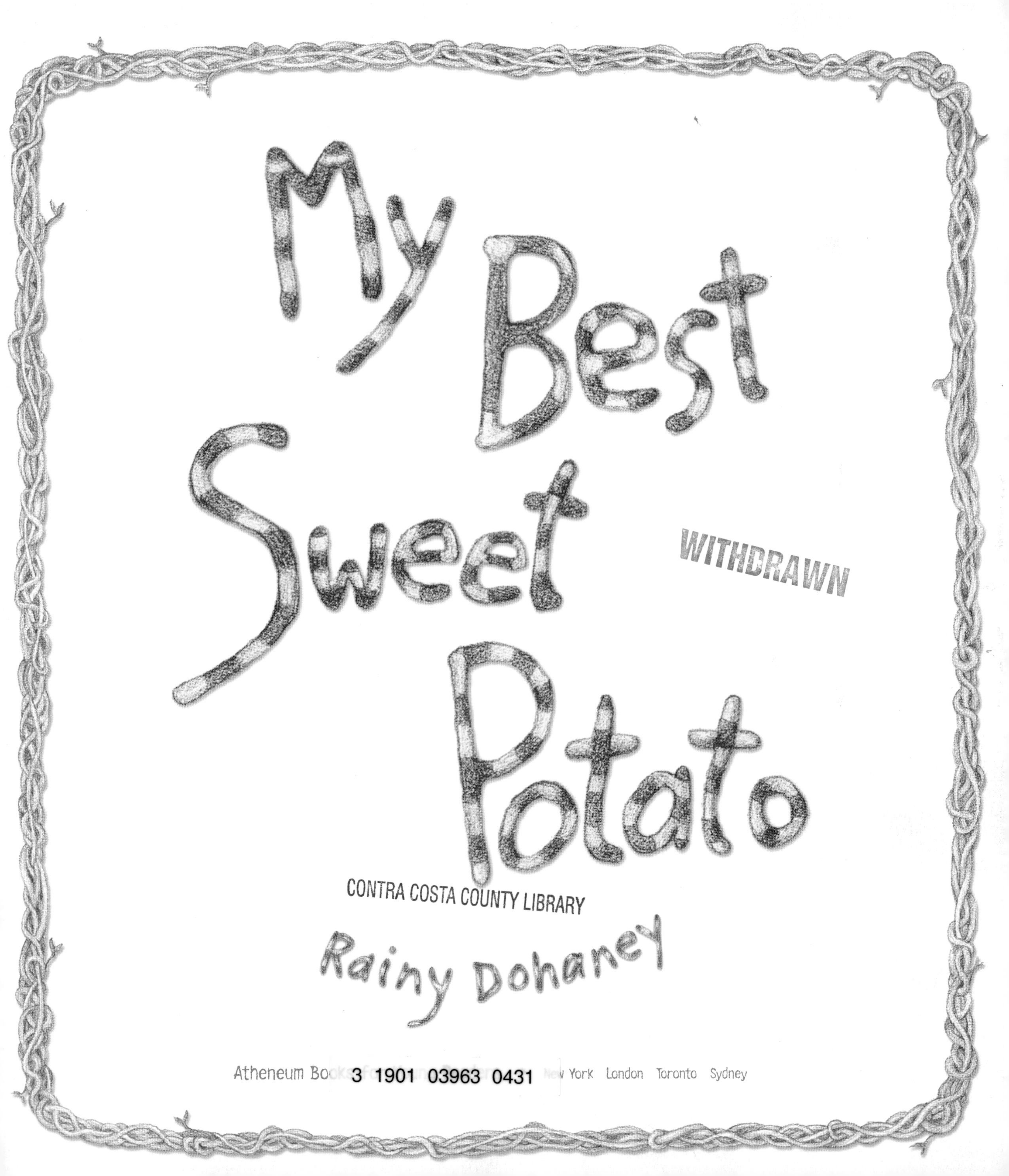

My Best Sweet Potato

Rainy Dohaney

Atheneum Bo New York London Toronto Sydney

K and her Woolyman did everything together.

They drew pictures together.

They had breakfast together . . .

and lunch . . .

and dinner.

They went swimming together.

They even raced turtles together.

A long time ago, when K was only three, Woolyman was an ordinary, everyday sort of Woolyman.

When K would pull his string, he'd say things like "Don't forget to brush your teeth," and "You're my best friend," and lots of other boring stuff.

Then one day
K's mother put
him in the washing
machine, and when
he came out,
he said,

"I have to go to the...

Sweet Potato,"

and he hasn't been
ordinary since.

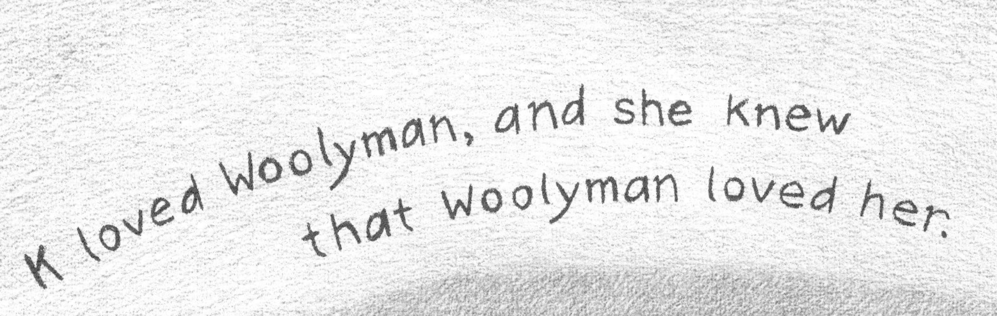

K loved Woolyman, and she knew that Woolyman loved her.

"You're my best . . .
Sweet Potato," he'd say.

Every Tuesday, K took Woolyman to feed Mr. Tree. She would sit her friend on his branch, and then run off to gather Mr. Tree's favorite food—rocks, of course.

One particular Tuesday, Mac, the weaverbird, was also out walking, gathering twigs and straw for his newest nest, when he noticed something perched nearby.

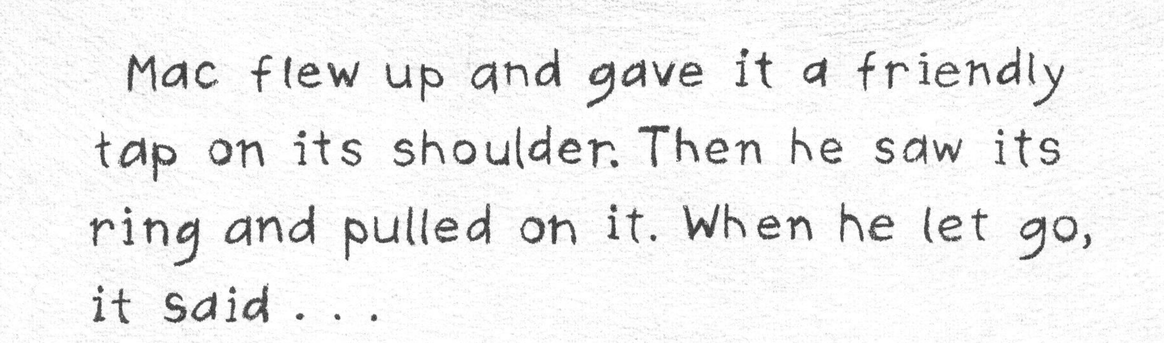

Mac flew up and gave it a friendly tap on its shoulder. Then he saw its ring and pulled on it. When he let go, it said . . .

"I'm afraid of the...**Sweet Potato!**"

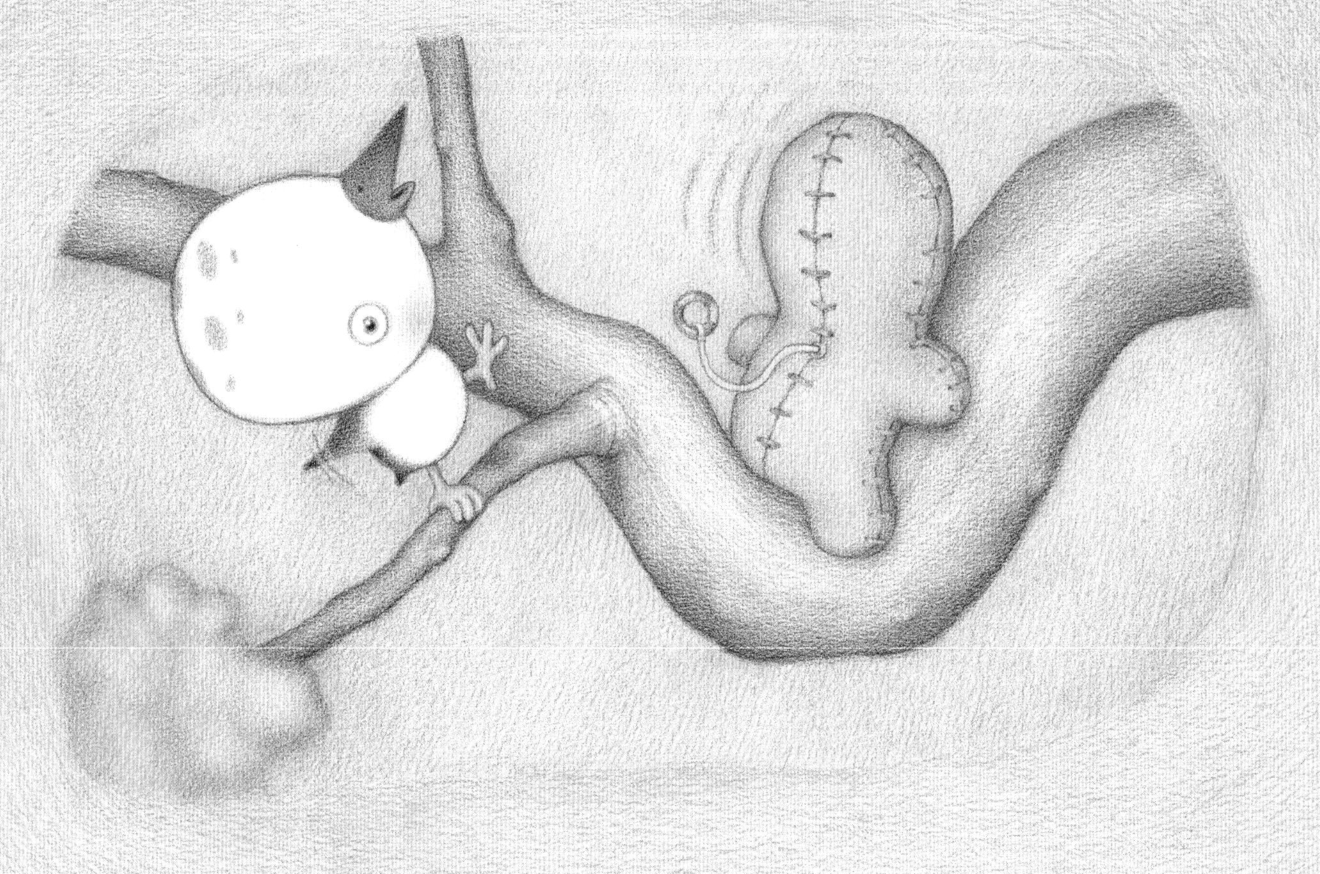

"Whoa! You scared the seeds out of me, fuzzy guy," squawked Mac, and he almost fell off his branch. "And if you're so afraid, why are you out here all by yourself?

Mac pulled the string again, and Woolyman answered, "You're my best... **Sweet Potato.**"

"Aw, gee, thanks, but we just met. Don't you have any friends?"

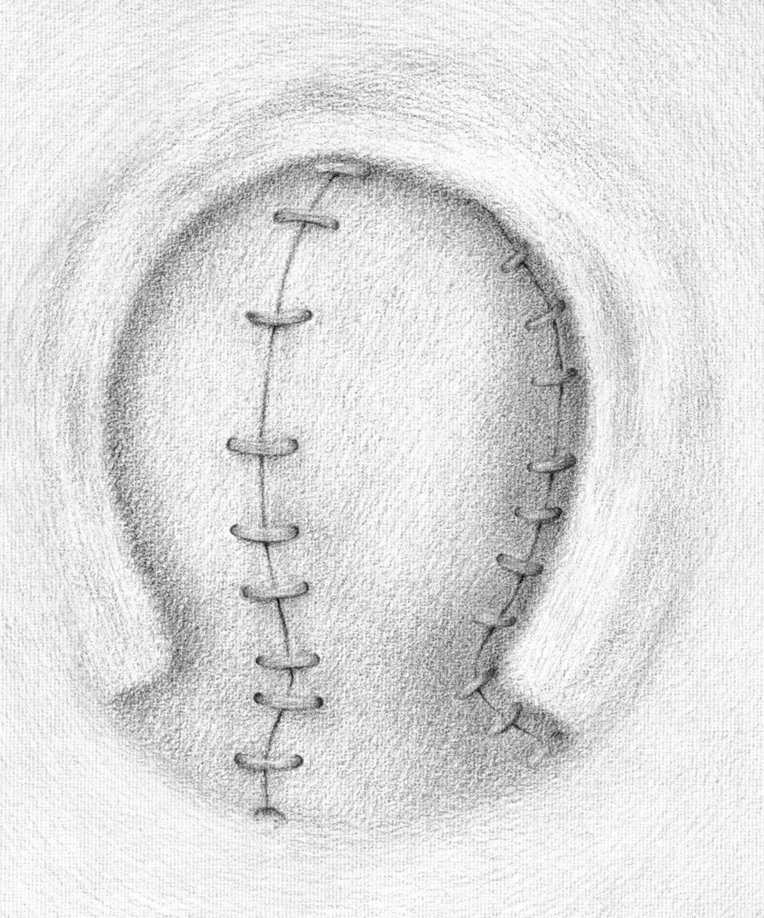

Mac pulled.

"Let's go for a . . .
Sweet Potato,"
Woolyman said.

"Sorry, I'm not hungry, buddy. I just ate," Mac replied. "But how would you like to come and see my newest projects?"

Woolyman grunted, "It's time for your . . .
Sweet Potato,"
which Mac took to mean, "I'd love to," and off they went.

Mac was excited to have a friend.

It wasn't long before K returned with food for Mr. Tree and a special racing turtle for her Woolyman. But when she looked up at his branch . . .

he was gone!

Maybe he fell, she thought,
and she searched the ground for him.

But
Woolyman
wasn't
there.

K sniffled a bit, and her chin started to quiver, and then, even though she didn't cry very often, she cried her eyes out.

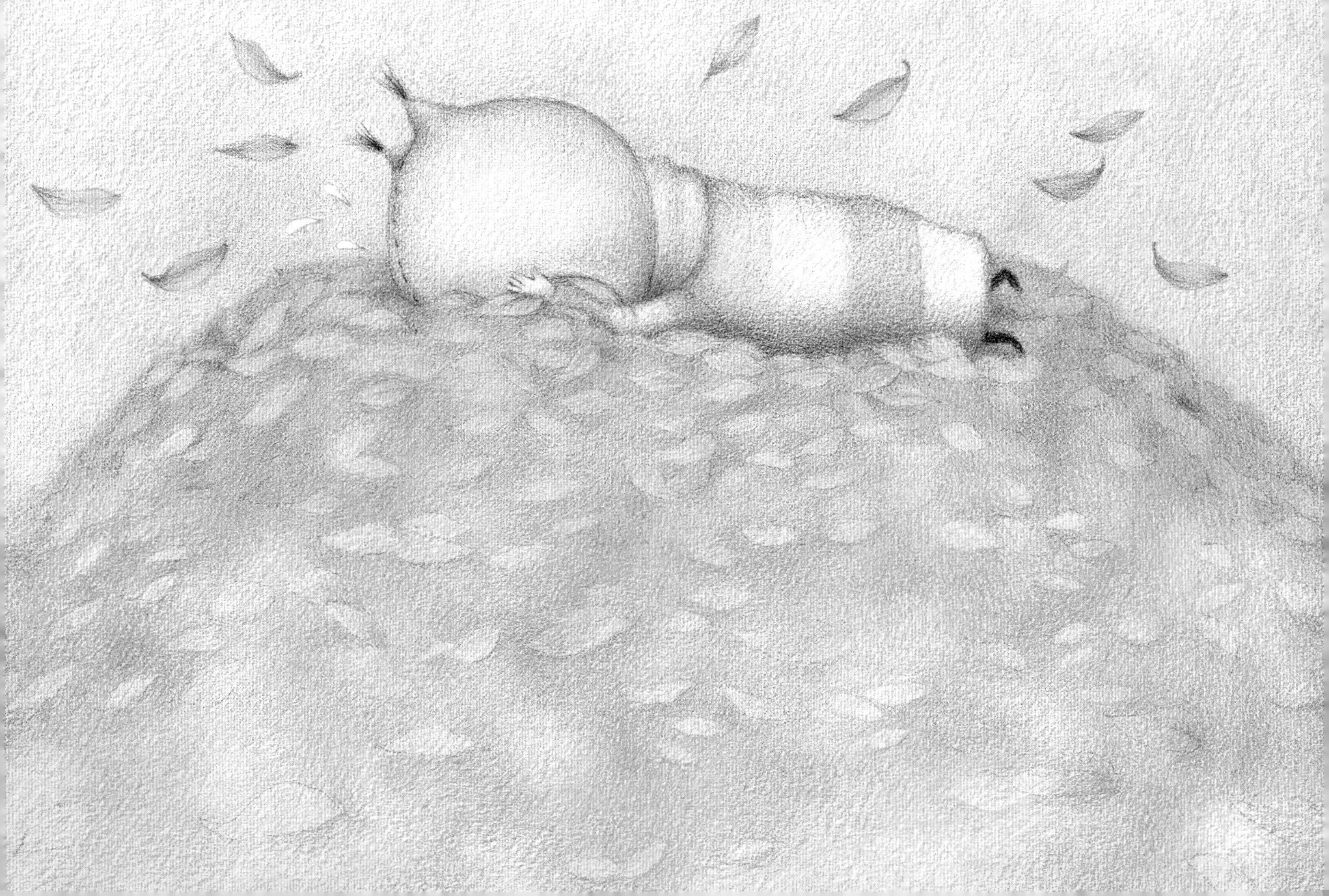

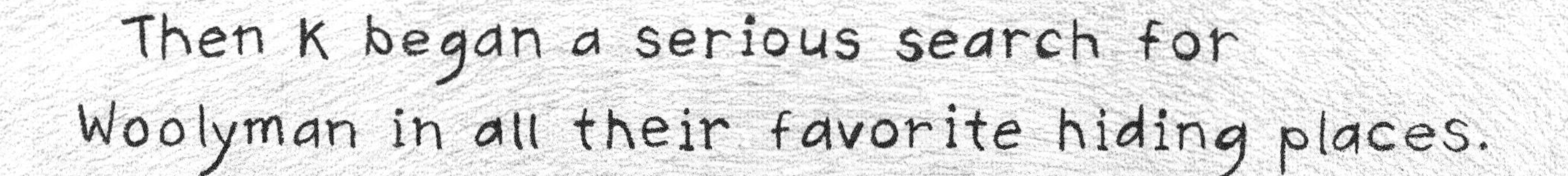

Then K began a serious search for Woolyman in all their favorite hiding places.

Nope.

Nope.

Nope.

Nope.

Nope.

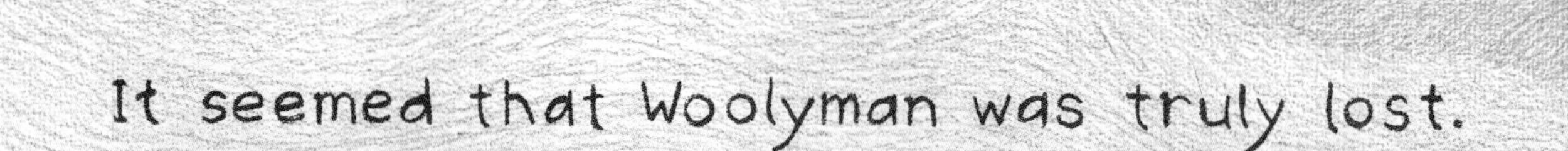

It seemed that Woolyman was truly lost.

Lunchtime had never been so lonely.

Meanwhile Mac
was busy showing
Woolyman all the
nests he had made.

"Whaddaya think, buddy?" he asked, and pulled Woolyman's string.

"Brown is my favorite . . . **Sweet Potato**," said Woolyman.

"Aw shucks, thanks." Mac looked fondly at his friend. "Hey, why don't I make you a nest of your own?"

Woolyman seemed to smile.

So Mac built Woolyman a comfy nest and placed his friend snugly inside.

"Which are better, dogs or cats?" he asked, making conversation.

He pulled Woolyman's string.

"What's your favorite . . . **Sweet Potato**?"

Woolyman grunted.

"C'mon, man, I asked you first," said Mac, laughing.

Just then, from behind
the bushes came a sound
like a sniffling piglet.

Mac snuck up closer and saw a little girl sobbing. "Hey, that's a picture of my fuzzy guy," he said to himself.

LOST

LOST

He looked back at his friend, Woolyman.

"Why didn't you tell me you had a home already?" Mac asked Woolyman.

But all that came out was "**Sweet Potato.**"

"Yeah, buddy, I feel the same way," said Mac quietly. "But you have to go home now."

Then Mac picked Woolyman up and carried him back to Mr. Tree. Gently he sat his friend back on the branch where he'd found him and whispered, "Don't be sad, fuzzy guy. I'll visit you every day."

Before Mac flew off, he pulled Woolyman's string one last time.

"Let's go
for a...
sweet
potato!"

K couldn't
believe her ears.
It was Woolyman,
right where she
had left him.
She grabbed him
off his perch
and squeezed him as
hard as she could.

Now lunch is never lonely, and turtle races are crazier than ever.

And when it's time for bed, K kisses Woolyman . . . and Woolyman just lies there.

But then K pulls that old string of his, and Woolyman says . . .

"You're my best... **sweet potato**."